DISNEY · PIXAR

FINDING NEMO

Adapted by Victoria Saxon

Illustrated by Scott Tilley

Designed by Disney's Global Design Group

 A Golden Book • New York

Copyright © 2003 Disney Enterprises, Inc./Pixar Animation Studios
All rights reserved under International and Pan-American Copyright Conventions. Published in the United States
by Golden Books, an imprint of Random House Children's Books, a division of Random House, Inc., New York,
and simultaneously in Canada by Random House of Canada Limited, Toronto. Golden Books,
A Golden Book, the G colophon, and the distinctive gold spine are registered trademarks of Random House, Inc.
Library of Congress Control Number: 2002113649
ISBN: 0-7364-2139-4
www.randomhouse.com/kids/disney
Printed in the United States of America

20 19 18 17 16 15 14 13 12

Now, most of you who are reading this book probably live above the sea . . .

. . . but others live underwater.

Nemo and his father, Marlin, lived underwater. They were clownfish.

Because they were clownfish,
they were small. But other fish
were big!

Marlin was scared of the big
fish, so he always kept Nemo
close to him, tucked safely
inside their little home.

But today was Nemo's first day of school!
He was very excited. On the way there he saw . . .

a spotted fish . . .

. . . and a striped fish.

He saw *angry* fish . . .

. . . and H_AP^PY fish.

Mr. Ray, the science teacher, took
Nemo's class on a field trip. Nemo
and his friends sneaked away and
swam to the really deep water.
Marlin chased after Nemo and
scolded him! Nemo was angry that
his father had embarrassed him in
front of his new friends . . .

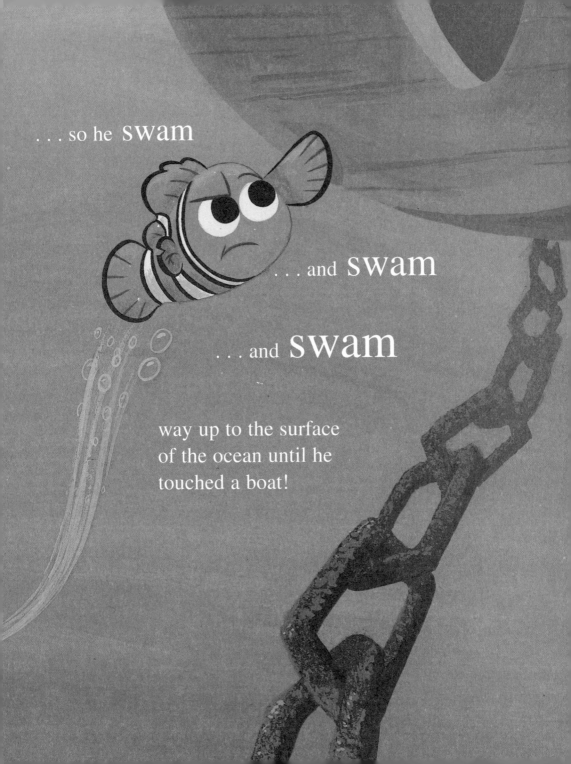

. . . so he **swam**

. . . and **swam**

. . . and **swam**

way up to the surface
of the ocean until he
touched a boat!

Then Nemo got caught!
"Daddy!" cried Nemo.
"Nemo!" cried Marlin.

Nemo was taken away in the boat. Marlin
tried to save his son, but the boat sped away
so fast it soon disappeared. Nemo was gone.
But Marlin would not give up. The only thing
on his mind now was finding Nemo.

Looking for help, Marlin swam into all sorts of fish. They pushed him and shoved him. They bumped into him. Soon Marlin was knocked aside.

One friendly fish named Dory swam down to
see if Marlin was okay. She was a little bit silly,
and she couldn't remember very much, but
she was happy to help Marlin!

Together, Dory and Marlin met a shark. Marlin was scared! But Dory thought it was very nice of the shark to invite them to a party.

The party was for sharks who were trying not to
eat fish. Luckily, they did not eat Marlin and Dory.

Marlin kept searching for Nemo. He and Dory found a scuba mask that belonged to the diver who had taken Nemo. They swam down into a very deep, dark place to get it.

Then they saw a light.

The light was attached to a mean anglerfish!
But it helped Dory read an address written on the
mask. Then the two friends swam away before
the anglerfish could eat them! Now Marlin knew
where to find Nemo: 42 Wallaby Way, Sydney.
Dory was so excited that she repeated the address
over and over . . . and over.

Next Marlin and Dory met some moonfish.
The moonfish made funny shapes.

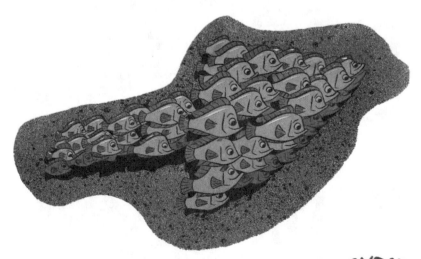

They pointed toward 42 WALLABY WAY, SYDNEY

Some friendly
turtles gave Marlin and Dory a ride.

Marlin told the
story of his search
for Nemo, and the
news spread across
the ocean!

Even Nemo heard about it at 42 Wallaby Way,
Sydney. He was very excited! He wanted to escape
from the fish tank where he was trapped.

Nemo's new friends were excited, too. The little
clownfish was bursting with pride. He had the bravest
dad in the sea!

Then a whale swallowed Marlin and Dory!
Dory told Marlin he didn't need to worry.
And she was right. The whale took them
as close as he could get to 42 Wallaby Way,
Sydney. In fact, he took them all the way to
Sydney Harbor!

At last a pelican named
Nigel helped Marlin and Dory
go straight to 42 Wallaby Way,
Sydney. But it was too late.
A little girl had grabbed Nemo.
Marlin couldn't save him!

Marlin was sad. He thought he would never see his son again.

But Nemo had escaped! Dory found him.

Father and son were overjoyed.

And when they finally returned home, both Nemo and Marlin were heroes.